To
Addison
May all your dreams &
wishes come true for
Christmas & forever

Hank M. Baker
2013

To my late wife Karen and to Susan, the two women in my life who gave me inspiration, motivation, and above all their love. With their support, this story emerged. I wish to thank my children, grandchildren and my great grandchildren for their patience and love while listening to all of "Gramps" Bricker's bedtime stories over and over again.

**The author, "Gramps Bricker"** is just another story telling grandparent who has seen his children, grandchildren, and now his great grandchildren voice their doubts upon seeing so many Santas everywhere without having a beard. During one Christmas season, H. Michael Bricker took his grandson Sean to visit Santa at a mall. Sean saw Santa putting on his beard and said, "Look Gramps, this Santa is a fake. That's not even a real beard!" Thus the idea for *The Christmas Santa Had No Beard* was born.

Read about Santa's adventures after he loses his beard, This not so jolly Santa asks, "Does a beard make me any different? Is trouble like this going to happen all night long?"

Children will find out why Santa loses his beard, the problems that ensue, and the surprising solution/ending.

*The Christmas Santa Had No Beard* will help restore the magical legend of Santa's image to every child. This story is destined to be one of the great Christmas classics of all time, and will be told and retold to generations and future generations.

**The illustrator, John Dall**, has said, "If I feel it.....I can create it."  John Dall's artistic drawings makes this story come even more alive. John is a Chicago based Native American artist and active participant in Ho-Chunk Indian affairs. He is a free-lance illustrator whose works have appeared in Tom Catalano's book *Tall Tales, And Short Stories*, *Brother Edwin*, and *The Carrier*.

**Book designer, Qi "Mary" Meng**, is an experienced web programmer and magazine designer from Shanghai, China. Her creativity in designing *The Christmas Santa Had No Beard* has extremely enhanced both the writing and illustrations in this work.

**Spanish translation by Ana Facio-Krajcer.** Special thanks to Dave, Halina, Judy, Ingrid,Bob, Rick Hall,Kathy and Michael Bricker.

**Electronic version compiled by Jean Bergeron,PH.D. Computer Science.** Canadian Information Productivity Awards for the MALICOTS Project in Institutions Category, (2001).  CEO of AMSO Software Company.

**Audio compilation completed by Dennis James,** sound engineer and professional photographer.

# The Christmas Santa Had No Beard

By H.M. "Gramps" Bricker

Illustrated by John Dall

It was the night before Christmas and all through Santa's snow covered village, everyone was busy, including the mouse. The elves were working joyfully, wrapping presents and putting the finishing touches on the games, books, and just about any toy a child could wish for.

Outside, Santa was checking the reins and harnesses on all the sleighs. Through the years, Santa needed to add extra sleighs because there are so many more children now than there were hundreds of years ago. As Santa finished, he hugged and kissed each reindeer before heading to his house.

Once inside, the scent of freshly baked Christmas cookies filled the air. A warm fire crackled in the fireplace and Christmas stockings hung from the mantle. Yes, there was a Christmas tree sparkling with lights and homemade ornaments, decorated in an old-fashioned way.

Santa's cheeks were still rosy red from the cold winter air and his long white hair covered his shoulders. His eyes twinkled like the lights on the tree and his beard was thick and very long, extending to his belt.

Mrs. Claus rocked back and forth in her chair mending Santa's red coat. Santa was busy rechecking his lists to make sure that no little boy or girl throughout the world could possibly be forgotten. He glanced up from his papers and exclaimed proudly, "Yes I believe that we didn't overlook a single child."

"Oh, Nicholas, there is one thing you did forget to do," Mrs. Claus declared. "Take a good look at yourself. You really need to have your hair and beard trimmed. I'll make an appointment for you at Baldy's, the elf's barber shop."

Santa walked over to the mirror, rubbed his long
beard and nodded his head. Just then, they heard
a knock on the door.

Mrs. Claus cried out, "Come in."

Speedy, the messenger, elf entered. Smiling and laughing, he took off his Christmas hat, bowed and declared, "Baldy the North Pole barber is waiting for you, Santa. He says you are four months late. Hmm, looking at your beard, I would say five."

"You're right, I really need a trim." Santa replied. He headed out the door and walked quickly to the barber shop.

As he opened the door, he was greeted with the sound of tiny little bells.

"Merry Christmas, Baldy," Santa said cheerfully.

"Baloney," grumbled Baldy. "Save all that Christmas talk. I just don't believe the stories about writing to Santa and having your Christmas wishes come true. I have been bald since I was a child, and wrote you year after year asking for hair. Each Christmas I received just toys and presents, but no hair. Look Santa, do you see any hair on the top of my head?"

"My good friend, you never mentioned this to me before. Perhaps my helpers overlooked it because hair is not a toy or a game. After all, it can't be wrapped as a present," Santa replied.

"That's all nonsense. Let's get down to barber shop business. How do you want your hair cut and your beard trimmed? Long? Close? Shaved?" Baldy asked. With his scissors in his hand, the barber continued, "Hey, how about a new, modern style for a change?"

"Yes. Yes. We want everyone to be happy," Santa muttered, thinking only about Baldy's hair disappointment. Santa yawned and laid back in the barber chair, immediately falling asleep. While Santa slept, the elf busily cut Santa's long hair.

Then he jumped on Santa's belly, and began cutting his long beard. He snipped Santa's beard here, and snipped some more there.

Baldy stepped back and examined his work. He shook his head, and continued trimming and cutting Santa's beard.

Baldy was just finishing as Santa began to wake up. Santa opened his eyes and he suddenly felt something cold and strange across his face. Santa's eyes scanned the floor around the barber chair. He saw the floor piled high with mounds and mounds of his white hair. Slowly Santa looked in the mirror, gasped, and cried out,

"Oh my gosh! SANTA CLAUS HAS NO BEARD!"

Shocked, Santa could not stop looking at his beardless face in the mirror. Rubbing his hands on his smooth, beardless face, Santa said, "Baldy, if you really want hair this Christmas, you will have it. That's a promise."

The elf grinned and answered, "While you were asleep, I thought what my life would be like if I did have hair. First of all, my shop would be called 'Hairy's' and not 'Baldy's North Pole Barber Shop'. My little baby girl would scream if she saw her daddy with long hair. Everyone would be confused. Sometimes, the things we wish for turn out to be not so important after all."

"That's very true. I guess we'll see what Mrs. Claus and the elves think of my new modern look. Thank you, and have a Merry Christmas, Baldy," Santa said, as he walked out of the barber shop.

On his way to feed the reindeer, Santa rushed past the North Pole Workshop. The reindeer were playing games, and seeing this beardless man, they immediately stopped moving and stood like frozen statues in the snow.

Santa reached out to pat their heads only to see the confused reindeer back away cautiously. The entire village suddenly became silent. Even the elves had stopped their singing, chattering and laughing.

Then, Santa heard a voice behind him shouting, "Hey mister, what are you doing? Why are you messing with Santa's reindeer on Christmas eve?"

Startled, Santa quickly turned his head. There he saw Pepe, manager of the toy operations, and all the elves from the North Pole Workshop, glaring at him angrily.

"Hello guys. It's me, Santa Claus! Gee whiskers! Don't you even recognize me?"

At that very moment, he felt something cold on his cheek. There was a reindeer's wet, red nose smack against his face.

"Ho! Ho!Ho!" Are you checking me out, also?" laughed Santa.

"You see, without your beard no one is ever going to believe that you are the real Santa Claus," Pepe declared.

"Yeah! Yeah!" The elves shouted out in agreement.

Hearing all the noise outside, Mrs. Claus opened the front door and walked out on the porch.

"Has anyone seen Santa around?" she asked.

"Yes, I certainly have! I am right here." answered Santa. Santa turned and looked up to face his wife.

"Oh my goodness! " She gasped, "Why would you pick today, of all days, to shave off your beard?"

Once again, Santa explained what happened at Baldy's barber shop. Santa remained outside busily directing the elves as they loaded the presents that were packed high and wide on the sleigh. Even Baldy was seen piling presents for Santa's trip. The elves were lining up on each side of the road waving their lanterns.

"All clear, Santa!" shouted one of the elves.

" Ho! Ho! Ho!" laughed Santa, "We are now ready for take off."

In no time at all, Santa visited hundreds and hundreds of homes, nibbling at every type of cookie. Everything proceeded right on schedule without a problem. Finally, as the sleigh landed on the rooftop of one house, Santa whispered to his reindeer, "This time I am going to bring you some treats also." And with a twinkling of his eye, Santa disappeared down the chimney, placing presents around the tree and filling the stockings with candy. Then he picked up a glass of milk and was trying to decide which one of the cookies he should eat. He finally selected a huge cookie and was about to put it in his mouth.

"Stop! Hey! What are you doing taking Santa's cookies and milk?" Startled, he turned his head and looked across the room. Staring at him were three very angry looking boys.

"Why boys, I am Santa! You must be Nathan because you are the oldest," he said with a hearty smile.

"Come on, you're a fake pretending to be Santa," said Sean, the next tallest boy.

"Yes, Santa has a beard and you don't," added the youngest.

"Well Todd, I know that this story may sound strange, but my barber shaved off my beard today. You believe me, don't you boys?" They all shook their heads.

"No way! You think you're tricky, but our names are on all the stockings," Nathan wisely replied.

The boys all broke out in laughter. Still laughing, Sean said, "Since it's Christmas, we feel that you should have your snack."

Then Todd said very sternly, "Yes, we'll just go back into the kitchen for more cookies and milk. We must have everything ready for the REAL Santa Claus you know, the one with the beard."

When the little boys came back into the room with more cookies and milk, the beardless Santa was gone. They found their presents under the tree and their stockings filled with candy. Then they heard the thumping of hoofs on the roof and the jingling of bells. When they looked out the window, they saw Santa's sleigh in the air. They also saw Santa holding the reins.

"There's Santa," they yelled. "And look, he has no beard!"

As Santa' sleigh flew across the sky, he was still rattled from his encounter with these boys.

This not so jolly Santa wondered, "Does a beard make me any different? Is trouble like this going to happen all night long?"

On his next stop, Santa quickly came down the chimney, and peered very cautiously around the room.  He raced over to the Christmas tree, threw the presents down, and hurriedly shoved candy in the stockings. Santa, hearing something behind him, turned his head very slowly. Suddenly, the evening silence was shattered.

A wide-eyed frightened little girl began crying out, "Mommy! Daddy! Wake up! Wake up! There's a man stealing our Christmas presents! Please, Hurry!"

Santa started to approach and calm her, and softly said,  "Oh Olivia, I..." Santa was never able to finish the sentence. Upstairs, he heard Olivia's sisters ordering the barking dog to attack. Then heard her father saying, "I'll get my shotgun!"

Racing down the stairs came the snarling dog with her father close behind. Santa ran toward the fireplace with the dog snapping at the seat of his red pants. Reaching the fireplace, he looked over his shoulder. The father had the shotgun raised, and the dog had a piece of Santa's red pants in his mouth.

"Merry Christmas everybody!" Santa shouted and he disappeared right up the chimney.

For the first time in Christmas history, Santa hesitated about making his next delivery. Slowly and sadly he got out of his sleigh. "Without my beard, nobody will ever believe that I am the real Santa Claus. Oh, how I wish I had a beard for Christmas," he moaned aloud.

Suddenly, a present that was lying on the front seat of the sleigh began to sparkle. It must be some of that special Christmas magic that happens this time of the year, he thought. Under the bright starlit sky, Santa saw his name on the package. Excited, he began unwrapping his present. All the reindeer jumped up and down with joy when they saw what was inside the box.

"Is it hair?" He wondered, "No, it's a BEARD! Isn't this wonderful! I am going to have a beard for Christmas! Ho! Ho! Ho! What a merry, merry Christmas," Santa shouted happily from the rooftop. As Santa put on his fake beard, he spotted a letter at the bottom of the box, and read it,

Dear Santa,
I hope that this gift comes in handy during holiday season. The hair on this beard is all yours. Please instruct your helpers that it is poss... to ...nd receive ... ...mas.
...mas,
...Baldy,
...Pole Barber

Dear Santa,

I hope that this gift comes in handy during the Holiday season. The hair on this beard is all yours. Please instruct your helpers that it is possible to wrap and receive hair for Christmas.

Merry Christmas,

BALDY, The North Pole Barber

This time it was a jolly, jolly Santa who climbed down the next chimney. When he finished filling the stockings and placing presents around the tree, he heard a snicker and then a silly giggle.

"Hi Santa, It's me," said the giggling voice.

"Hi, Moriah, Merry Christmas, I know that you have been a good little girl," beamed Santa.

The little girl reached over and touched Santa's beard, gave him a kiss, and then giggling ran right up the stairs.

"Good night," she yelled happily.

"Ho! Ho! Ho!" Santa chuckled, "And what a very merry Christmas it is!"

All through the night, in every country throughout the world, little children peeked from behind chairs, stairs, and everywhere else, and knew that the real Santa had visited them. What they never realized was that this was one Christmas that Santa did not have a beard.

And so children everywhere, heed these words of advice. Whenever you see a Santa Claus, and you think that his beard might not be real, remember he just might be the REAL Santa Claus who has received another super close shave from Baldy, the North Pole Barber.

THE END